FATHER FIGURES

TINA'S FIRST DANCE

**WRITTEN BY
REQUILL PHILLIPS**

ILLUSTRATED BY
JASMINE MILLS

Copyright © 2019 Mentor Select Publishing

Published 2020 by Mentor Select Publishing

Author Requill Phillips

Illustrator Jasmine Mills

Editor Tracy Hundley

ISBN: 978-1-950715-08-4

Printed in the United States of America

First Edition, February 2020

info@derrichphillips.com

www.father-figures.com

THIS BOOK BELONGS TO:

_____

_____

Tina loved school and her teacher thought she was one of the brightest students in her class. Tina read a lot of books, but math and science were her favorite subjects.

Every day she was eager to get to school to learn as well as to see her friends and teacher.

When she arrived at school one day, there was a big poster on the wall announcing a father-daughter dance. Tina instantly became sad and was distracted for the rest of the day in school.

Tina's mom noticed the change in her normally happy and bubbly daughter when she came home from school. Her mom gave her a huge hug and asked, "What's the matter, love?"

Tina replied sadly, "My school is having a father-daughter dance but I don't have a dad to take me." Tina had lost her father a couple years earlier and now she had only her mom and her brother, Larry.

Tina's mom responded, "That doesn't mean you can't go. I know many great father figures who would be honored to take you to the dance and teach you lessons a father teaches his daughter."

A giant smile appeared across Tina's face. Her mother continued, "I will take you to meet them so you can ask questions and decide who you would have the most fun with at the dance."

Tina asked, "Like an interview?"

"Exactly like an interview," her mother responded. "We will do it this weekend while your brother is on his camping trip."

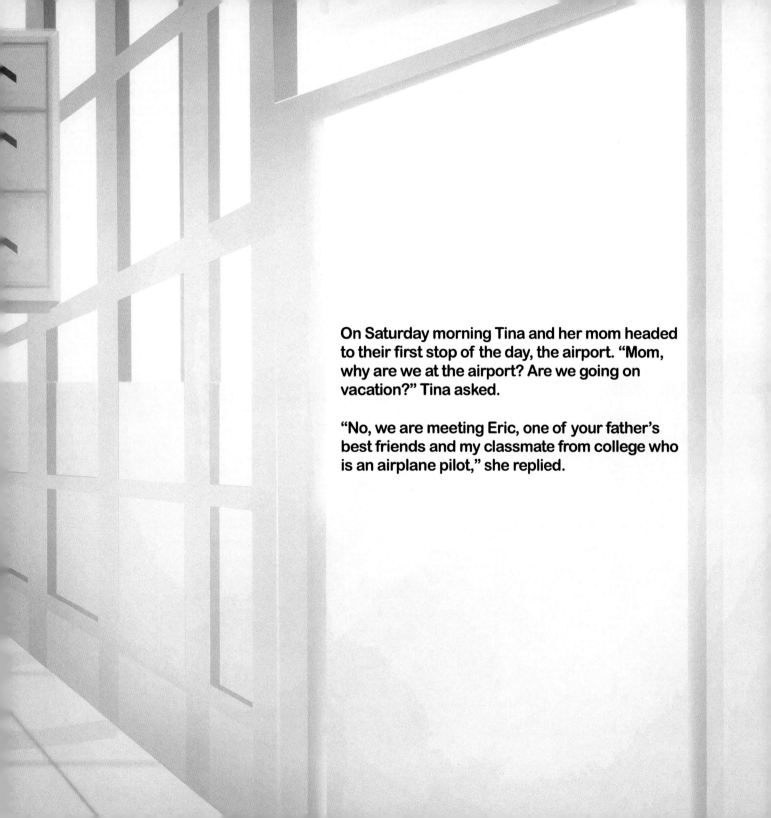

On Saturday morning Tina and her mom headed to their first stop of the day, the airport. "Mom, why are we at the airport? Are we going on vacation?" Tina asked.

"No, we are meeting Eric, one of your father's best friends and my classmate from college who is an airplane pilot," she replied.

They approached a tall man dressed in a dark suit with a crisp white shirt and pilot hat that looked familiar from pictures Tina had seen in an old photo album at home.

Eric shook Tina's hand and said, "I haven't seen you since you were a tiny baby." He then took them both on a tour of the cockpit of the airplane he captained.

Tina was amazed by all the buttons, screens, and levers. She asked Eric many questions about being a pilot, his family, whether he was a good dancer, and many other subjects. Then she asked a very important question. "What would my father want you to teach me?"

After thinking about it for a few seconds, Eric said, "How to follow your dreams. It required great perseverance to become a pilot. Many people thought I should pick an easier career. Instead I believed in myself when others didn't, and now I get to do something I love."

Tina and her mom thanked Eric for his time and waved goodbye as they drove away, heading to their second stop of the day. "Who are we going to see now?" Tina asked her mom.

"Your dad's brother, Uncle Chris, at his restaurant," she replied.

"Yummy!" Tina exclaimed. "Because I'm hungry!"

"Uncle Chris!" Tina yelled with excitement.

"How's my favorite niece?" Chris asked excitedly as they hugged.

"I'm great! We just saw dad's old friend Eric at the airport," Tina said.

"Your mom didn't tell me I was going to have to compete to take you to your school dance," he joked. "Guess I better hope teaching you your dad's favorite recipe will score me some points."

"What are we making today?" Tina asked.

"Gumbo," Uncle Chris replied.

Both began to wash and chop the ingredients needed to make the dish. While they worked, Tina asked her uncle many questions: Why did he want to become a chef? What was his favorite meal to cook? What would he wear to the dance if they went?

Then Tina asked, "Why do you think gumbo was my dad's favorite dish?"

"The ingredients of gumbo taste good by themselves, but when you combine all those textures and flavors, they work as a team to create something better than the individual ingredients," Uncle Chris replied. "In my role as chef, many people have to work together to create one meal. Your father would have wanted me to teach you the importance of team work, and what could be a better way to teach teamwork than by making gumbo?"

Once the meal was complete, they ate the gumbo they had prepared and talked for a while until Tina's mom reminded Tina that they had one more stop for the day.

"Where to next, mom?" Tina asked.

"We are actually going to make a pit stop so I can get my car oil changed," her mom responded.

"Seriously? But we were having so much fun," Tina said, disappointed.

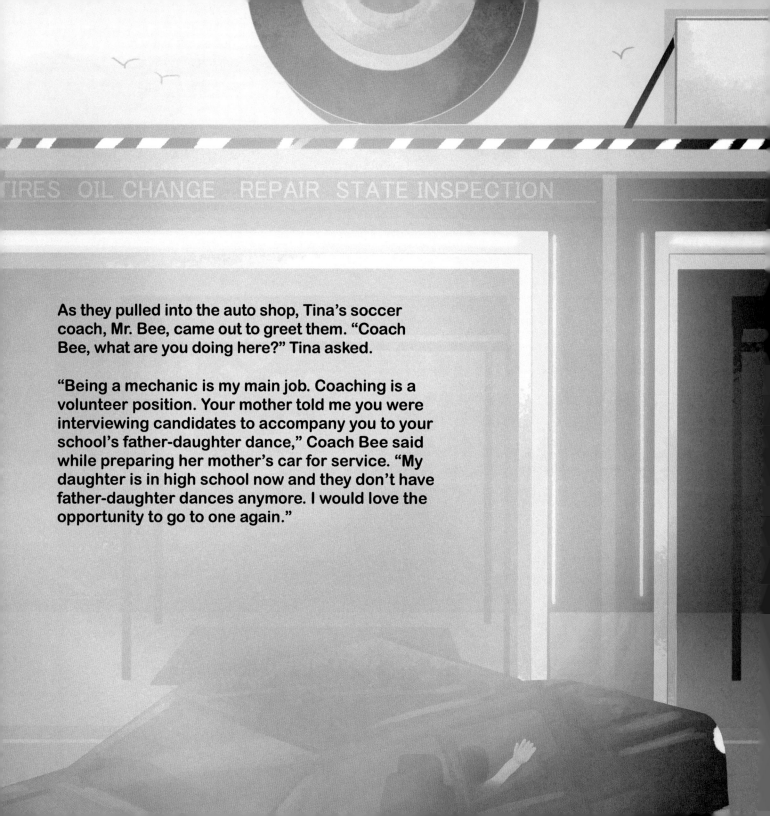

As they pulled into the auto shop, Tina's soccer coach, Mr. Bee, came out to greet them. "Coach Bee, what are you doing here?" Tina asked.

"Being a mechanic is my main job. Coaching is a volunteer position. Your mother told me you were interviewing candidates to accompany you to your school's father-daughter dance," Coach Bee said while preparing her mother's car for service. "My daughter is in high school now and they don't have father-daughter dances anymore. I would love the opportunity to go to one again."

"That's a kind offer, Coach Bee," Tina said.

"I just have a few questions."

Tina began pointing to the different car parts and asking what each did. She asked Coach Bee what his favorite car was and what type of dress his daughter wore to her father-daughter dances. Then she asked, "Did you teach your daughter how to change a tire?"

"I sure did, because I want my daughter to know she is capable of doing anything her brothers can do. I'm raising a strong, independent young lady," he said.

"Could you please show me how to change a tire since my dad can't teach me?" Tina asked.

"Of course," Coach Bee responded, handing her protective glasses and gloves.

When the tire was changed, Tina and her mom said thank you and headed home.

"It's time to wake up!" Tina's mother called. "We have a busy Sunday ahead of us after church."

"Are we doing more interviews for the father-daughter dance?" Tina asked.

"We sure are!" her mother exclaimed.

Tina leaped from bed and headed to the bathroom to shower, brush her teeth, and get dressed for church.

After church Tina and her mother got in the car and her mother started driving. They were turning down streets that looked very familiar to Tina. "I think I know where we are going," Tina said.

"Oh, really, Miss Smarty Pants?" her mom asked with a smile.

"Yep! Grandma and Grandpa's house," Tina said happily. As soon as her mom parked in front of her grandparent's house, Tina flung open the car door and ran inside as fast as she could.

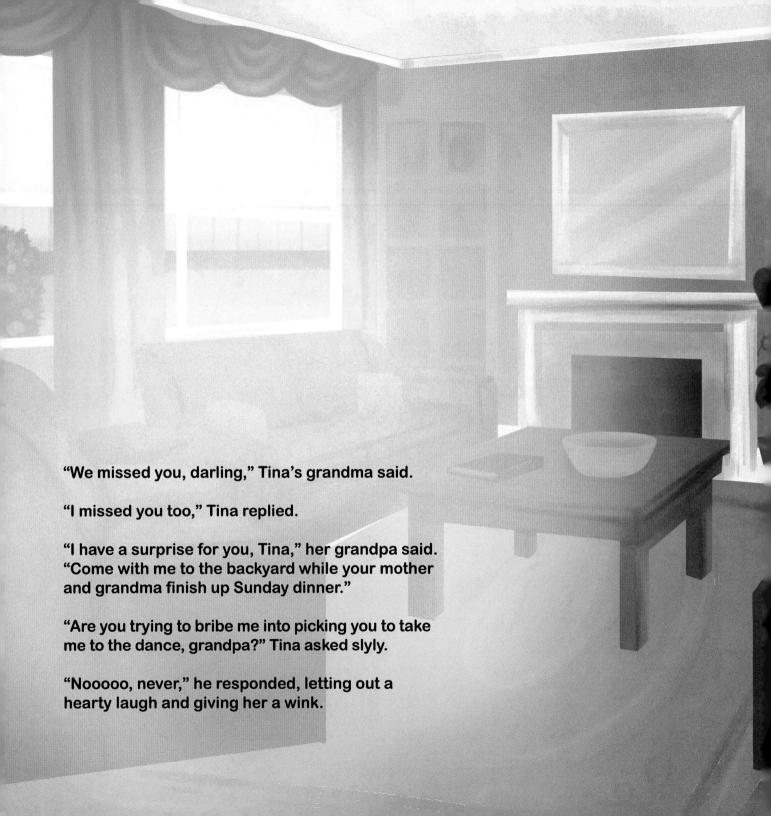

"We missed you, darling," Tina's grandma said.

"I missed you too," Tina replied.

"I have a surprise for you, Tina," her grandpa said. "Come with me to the backyard while your mother and grandma finish up Sunday dinner."

"Are you trying to bribe me into picking you to take me to the dance, grandpa?" Tina asked slyly.

"Nooooo, never," he responded, letting out a hearty laugh and giving her a wink.

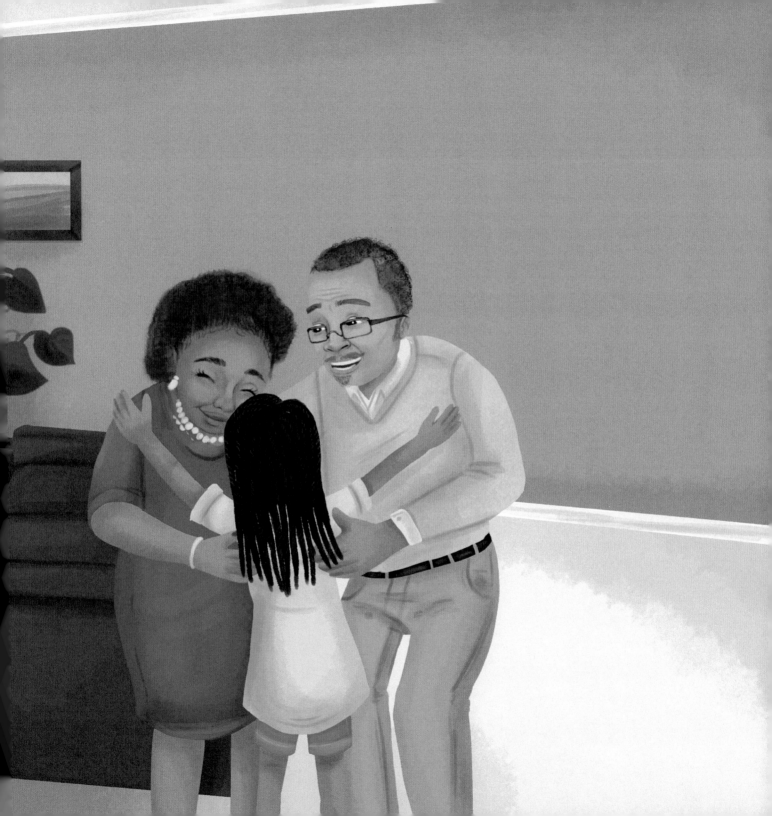

"When did you get a shed in the backyard? What's inside it?" Tina asked.

"You know, I was a construction worker for years before I retired. I built that shed for your grandma as a birthday gift so she could store all her gardening tools."

"That was so thoughtful of you, grandpa. I'm sure she loves it," Tina replied.

"She does." He continued, "I was thinking we could use this extra wood to build a bird house together."

"I would love to, grandpa!" Tina exclaimed.

The two got busy measuring, cutting, and nailing the wood together to make a bird house. While they worked, Tina asked her grandpa many questions. Did he miss working as a construction worker? What was the biggest building he had built? What color suit would he wear to the dance? And then she asked, "Why do you always do so many nice things for grandma even when it's not her birthday?"

"Because I love and respect her," grandpa responded. "I want her to know I would do anything in the world for her, so I show her that daily through my actions. My hope is that I'm teaching you through my actions how your husband should treat you one day."

Once they finished building the bird house, Tina and her grandpa cleaned up the area and themselves for dinner. Tina's mom and grandma had cooked a delicious, healthy meal for them to enjoy. Everyone talked and laughed together, enjoying the quality family time.

"Tina, we have to leave for our final interview," her mother said.

"But we haven't had dessert yet!" Tina whined.

"You can have one cookie from the cookie jar, and then you have to do as your mother says," Tina's grandma said.

Tina kissed her grandparents on the cheek, said goodbye, and then grabbed a cookie and her bird house and headed toward the door. She noticed her mom had packed a bag of leftover food. "Is that food for Larry when he gets back from camping?" Tina asked.

"You will find out who it is for soon enough," her mom replied.

As they drove, Tina stared out her window, looking up at the bright stars in the dark sky. She started wondering where they were headed next, but before she got lost in her thoughts, they were pulling up to the hospital.

"Mom, I only had one cookie. I don't have a tummy ache," Tina said.

"Relax," her mom replied after laughing. "We are here to see your Uncle Simon. He has to work late tonight and your grandma wanted me to bring him dinner." Uncle Simon was her mother's big brother.

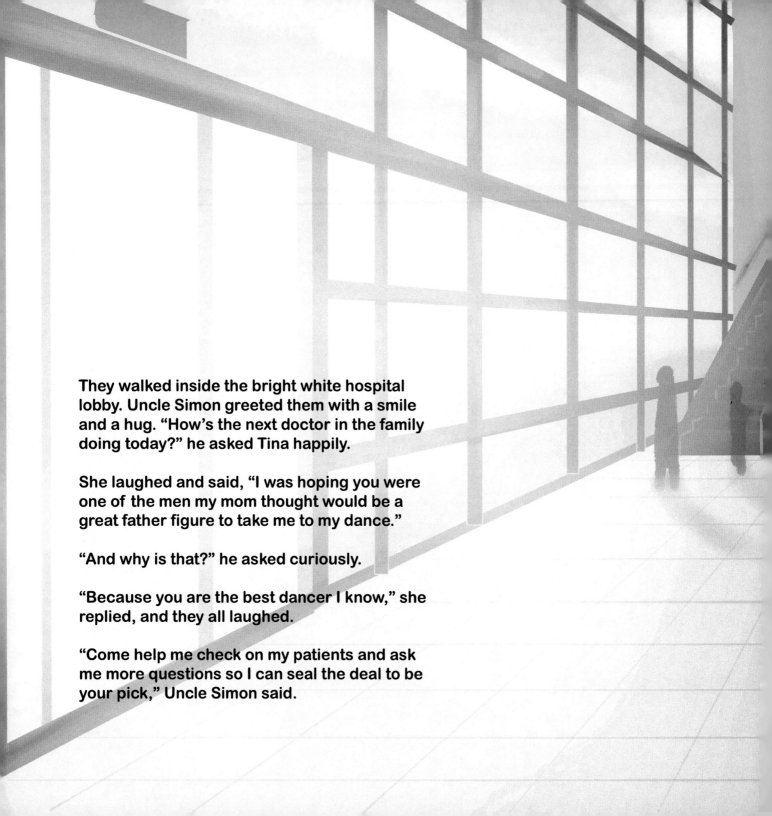

They walked inside the bright white hospital lobby. Uncle Simon greeted them with a smile and a hug. "How's the next doctor in the family doing today?" he asked Tina happily.

She laughed and said, "I was hoping you were one of the men my mom thought would be a great father figure to take me to my dance."

"And why is that?" he asked curiously.

"Because you are the best dancer I know," she replied, and they all laughed.

"Come help me check on my patients and ask me more questions so I can seal the deal to be your pick," Uncle Simon said.

Uncle Simon and Tina went to several patients' rooms to ask them how they were feeling. Between visiting patients, Tina asked her uncle many questions. She wanted to know how long he had to go to school to become a doctor, who taught him how to dance so well, and why he wanted to become a doctor. Then she asked, "What would you teach me if I were your daughter?"

"Always help others whenever you can because it's better to be selfless instead of selfish," he responded. "You don't have to be a doctor to save lives. There are so many small things you can do to brighten someone's day."

"Was your day brightened when we brought you dinner?" Tina asked.

"It sure was," Uncle Simon said, grinning widely.

They headed back down to the lobby where Tina's mother was waiting. Everyone said their goodbyes and Tina and her mother headed home.

That night as Tina lay in bed, she thought about the huge decision she had to make about who she would ask to the dance. All the men were wonderful and had many things they could teach her.

She would love to learn more about following her dreams from Captain Eric. Spending time with Uncle Chris learning more about team work sounded great too. Learning how to be independent, like Coach Bee was raising his daughter, was also very important. Just as important was learning from her grandpa how she should be treated by her future husband. But dancing all night with Uncle Chris and learning different ways to help others could be fun too.

Finally, Friday night arrived. The night of the dance. After almost a week of trying to decide who she wanted to take her to the father-daughter dance, Tina had made her decision. She was wearing the beautiful dress her mother bought her, and her mom had styled her hair to look extra pretty.

"You look beautiful, baby," her mother said.

"Thank you," Tina replied, just as the doorbell rung.

Tina opened the door with her mother's permission and in walked Captain Eric, Uncle Chris, Coach Bee, Grandpa, and Uncle Simon.

Tina beamed. "I want to thank you all for agreeing to take me to my dance. After interviewing each of you, I realized all of you are great father figures!" She grinned at the men and continued, "I invited you all because I wanted to do something to help other people, like Uncle Simon taught me. There are other girls in my class without dads. Now, with all of you going, they will have father figures to dance with too!"

Everyone smiled and they all headed to the dance.

Tina had one of the best nights of her life. She danced the night away and so did all of her classmates.

THE END

Requill Phillips, PMP is a wife, mother, author, YouTuber, and marketing maven. A native of Toledo, Ohio she earned a Bachelor of Arts degree in Communications from the University of Toledo. She is passionate about creating art and stories that positively impact the lives of others. Requill currently resides in Dallas, Texas with her husband Derrich Phillips, daughter Legacy, and "dogter" Empress.

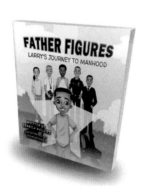

If you enjoyed this book please leave us a review on Amazon and check out the other book in the Father Figures series. Visit www.father-figures.com to claim your exclusive bonus offers.

Made in the USA
Monee, IL
10 April 2020